Rusty

Rag

Tufty

Mufty

Misty

Rusty

Rag

Tufty

Mufty

Misty

For my Aunt Joan, who gave me poetry books
~ CW

For 'Meraviglio' with tenderness
~ SF

SIMON AND SCHUSTER

First published in Great Britain in 2006 by Simon and Schuster UK Ltd
Africa House, 64-78 Kingsway, London WC2B 6AH

This paperback edition first published in 2006

Book designed by Genevieve Webster
The text for this book is set in Nicolas-Jensen
The illustrations for this book are rendered in acrylic

A CIP catalogue record for this book is available from the British Library upon request

ISBN 1 416 90486 7
EAN 9781416904861

Printed in China
1 3 5 7 9 8 6 4 2

Chicken for Supper

Carrie Weston & Sophie Fatus

SIMON AND SCHUSTER

London New York Sydney

On a clear, moonlit night Mummy Fox kissed
each of her five children goodbye.
"We will have chicken for supper tonight!" she told them.
The little foxes licked their lips and their tummies rumbled.
"Now, do not leave the den when I am gone,"
warned Mummy Fox.
"No, Mummy! We'll be good, Mummy!" sang the five
little foxes together.

Then they waved their little white paws as Mummy Fox
disappeared into the night.

The five little foxes all
huddled together: Tufty, Mufty,
Rusty, Misty and Rag.
They waited and they thought
of chicken for supper.

They waited and they waited.

"Let's go and play!" said Rag.
"But Mummy said not to leave the den," said Tufty.
"What if we just poked our noses out?" suggested Mufty.
"It's very dark out there," squeaked Rusty
and Misty together.
The five little foxes waited some more.

"Well, *I'm* off to have fun," yelled Rag suddenly,
as he darted out of the den and into the night.
His brothers and sisters watched him go.

"Mummy will be cross," said Misty.

"I do hope he'll be all right," said Rusty.

"Maybe we should follow him," said Tufty.

Each little fox crept nearer and nearer the hole to their den.
They sniffed the air. They looked at each other.
Then, one by one, they leapt out into the night.
First Tufty, then Mufty, Rusty and Misty.
"*Wheee!*" they shouted as they slid
down the bank after Rag.

They jumped.

They romped.

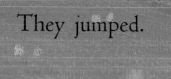

They rolled.

They tumbled.

They crept and they leapt.

Suddenly Tufty stopped.

"Just look at our muddy coats!" she said.

"And our dirty white socks!"

"Let's just go a little bit farther," pleaded Rag.

"It's so dark," squeaked Rusty.

"And scary!" whispered Misty.

"One of us could get lost!" said Mufty.

"One of us could *already* be lost –
I can't see a thing!" laughed Rag.

Misty put her paws over her eyes.

"Oh no!" she cried. "One of us is lost in the dark!"

The little foxes began to weep.

"One of us is lost in the dark!" they wailed.

Tufty wiped her eyes and sniffed.

"I'm the oldest," she said, "so I shall count us all."

The little foxes lined themselves up in front
of their big sister. She tapped each of their noses
in turn as she counted.

"One," she said, tapping Mufty's nose.

"Two," she said as she tapped Rusty.

"Three," she went on as she tapped Misty.

"Four," she said as she got to Rag.

Then she stopped.

"Four!" gasped Tufty, "I've only counted to four!
Oh dear! One of us *is* lost."

The little foxes wailed and wept some more.

Then Mufty dabbed his nose.

"Let me count," he said. "I'm the second oldest."

The little foxes all lined up in front of Mufty.
He tugged each of their tails as he counted.
"One." He tugged Tufty's tail.
"Two." He grabbed Rusty's tail.
"Three." He gave a pull on Misty's tail.
"Four." He yanked Rag's bushy tail
with the white tip.

"Oh my buttons!" wailed Mufty.
"We used to be five and now we're only four!"

The little foxes' wailing grew
louder and louder.
"Mummy will be so cross!"
whimpered Misty.

"I wish I knew how
to count," wailed Rusty.

Just then there was a rustling noise.
A flapping noise. A clucking noise.
Mrs Chicken appeared from under a bush.
"Cluck, cluck, cluck," she said kindly,
"what is all this crying?"

"One of us is missing," sniffed Tufty.

"Our mummy told us not to go out," cried Mufty.

"We used to be five and now we're four," stuttered Rusty.

"One of us is lost in the night," wept Misty.

"It's all my fault!" wailed Rag.

Mrs Chicken clucked and fussed over the little foxes.

She brushed the mud off their fine red coats. She combed out
their whiskers. She blew all their noses and wiped their eyes.
"There, there, there," she clucked softly as she checked their paws.

Then Mrs Chicken gently stood the little foxes in a row
and patted each of their heads as she counted out loud.
"One." She patted Tufty first.
"Two." Then Mufty.
"Three." Next Rusty.
"Four." And Misty.
"Five. There." She patted Rag last.

"You've found one of us!" yelped Tufty.

"You've saved us!" barked Rag.

"Thank you! *Thank you!*" yapped all the little foxes at once.

Mrs Chicken led all the little foxes back to their den.

"Come along now," she clucked. "Hurry, hurry at the back."

The hole at the top of the den was dark.

"Won't you come in with us?" asked Rusty.

"We're scared," said Misty.

"*Please,*" begged Rag.

"Well, just for a minute or two then," said Mrs Chicken.
Deep, deep down into the hole she went.

At the bottom of the den two eyes gleamed.

Sharp white teeth sparkled.

Whiskers twitched.

A wet nose sniffed the air.

"Mummy! Mummy!" yelped all the little foxes together.
"Where have you been?" asked a worried Mummy Fox.
The little foxes all began talking at once.

Mummy Fox listened to their story as she stirred
a steaming pot on the fire.
"We're hungry," said Rag at last.
"I'm not surprised," said Mummy Fox, "and all
I've brought tonight are vegetables from the farmer's field . . ."

Mrs Chicken looked at Mummy Fox.

Mummy Fox looked at Mrs Chicken.

". . . But I've made a lovely soup," smiled Mummy Fox,
"and there's plenty to go round."
Mummy Fox stirred the soup and Tufty counted out
the bowls for each of them.

"One. Two. Three. Four. Five. Six . . .

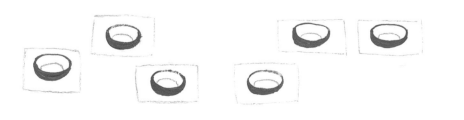

"Seven!"

So the little foxes did have a chicken for supper that night.
And she enjoyed the soup very much indeed.

Rusty

Rag

Tufty

Mufty

Misty

Rusty

Rag

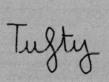

Tufty

Mufty

Misty